BLACK DUST

ALI SEAY

Tiny Terrors

CONTENT NOTES

*For a list of potentially triggering content,
please skip to page 57.*

BLACK DUST
ALI SEAY

"Where do you come from?" the waitress asks. She tries not to stare as I wipe my hands, fruitlessly, on my filthy jeans.

I'm used to this question. I always tell the truth. It's all I know.

"An orphanage in San Antonio, Texas," I say.

She pours coffee into my cup and tells me my food will be out soon.

At the moment, I work in a rock quarry. It helps to be able to say I work in a dusty environment, given my appearance.

It will be time to move on soon because the dust is turning darker, like soot. Nearly black, and black is never good.

Obviously, I don't remember my infanthood, but Sister Mary told me I was dropped off as a baby. In a filthy little cradle. Only after multiple baths and comparing notes did the nuns realize I generated the dust myself. That I hadn't been mistreated. I produced it.

Sister Mary decided to completely douse me in Holy Water a few months after I arrived.

It didn't stop the dust—nor the bad things that had started to crop up around us, for that matter—but it did tame it. Made it manageable. The bad things were related, too, they thought. The orphanage seemed immune to some degree. But for those who came in contact with us, the surrounding neighborhood? Bad things happened.

The waitress plunks my food down and takes a step back as if my dust is contagious. It's not. But it can easily get on her, and that would be gross, so I don't take offense.

"Anything else?" she asks.

I consider asking for some Wet Naps to amuse myself but simply shake my head and say thanks.

She hurries off, her relief evident.

I dig into my bacon, eggs, and toast, entirely used to the dust that sifts down off me and into my food. People stare, but I'm wearing my quarry tee, so I hope that helps them assume I'm just a grimy worker who just got off work.

I eat my food mechanically, drink my coffee, and block everyone out while trying to decide where to go now that it's about to get bad. I need a certain kind of job to live like this without suspicion. Garbage man, maintenance man, a dump worker, and the like. I need a very dirty environment. It helps disguise me. As far as human relationships, it's pretty much me, myself, and I—and the occasional sex worker I hire when the cycle starts fresh and the dust is barely noticeable.

I eat the last bite of toast just as a man wearing a mask enters, waving a gun and barking at the waitress who served me. I feel heavy inside. I watch. I wait. There's nothing I can do.

He demands money.

She screams.

She attempts to do what he says.

He shoots her anyway.

I look down at my hands and the table and my jeans. Black dust. Everywhere. Thicker.

Time to go.

I toss a ten on the table and get up and walk out in the middle of the drama.

I'm in no danger.

They won't hurt me.

They never do.

***

At age eighteen, the orphanage had to oust me. Sister Mary told me she could hide me. I could live nearby. That the nuns wouldn't desert me the way my real family had. But I wanted a shot at a life. Or maybe I hoped that getting out of San Antonio, going north, would somehow allow me to run from the filth of my life.

I quickly learned that wasn't possible.

I got a job at a dump, worked it out with the manager to secretly live in a small shack on premises for a small reduction in pay (that he secretly kept). My job made my appearance fairly easy to explain.

That had been in Maine. When the dust eventually went black, I was at the post office to mail a bill. A disgruntled worker decided that was the perfect day to shoot up the place, killing five co-workers and two customers.

I was, of course, unscathed.

I went home, showered, and dried off. My appearance then looked fairly normal. Just a little bit of light gray dust on my body here and there.

It was time to move on. So, I shut the place up, went to town, hired some female company, and had a few beers at a bar while I was still at the stage where no one paid attention to me or my dust.

That night, I drove south. I ended up in Pennsylvania.

"And now it's time to go," I say aloud to myself. I talk to myself a lot.

I go down to the bar and look for a new girl. One who's never been with me. I order a drink, and the bartender says, "Hey, Joe! Looking snazzy. Got a date?"

He's never seen me so clean. Unfortunately, this means he'll never see me again.

"Not yet, but here's hoping," I say, raising my beer.

She must catch the exchange, because a tall, dark-haired beauty with big, blue eyes walks over a few minutes later.

"Would you like to buy me a drink?" she asks.

I smile. "I'll buy you a drink if you'll accompany me to my motel room in a while."

I'm not crazy about the fact that I always end up with professionals, but it makes life easier. No normal woman would understand my cycle. And no normal woman would want to touch me most of the time.

"I thought you were a local. The bartender knew you by name."

"I am, but I'm getting ready to move."

Satisfied that I'm not a traveling serial killer, she sidles closer. "When are you moving?"

"Tomorrow morning," I say. "Want to wish me bon voyage?"

Her vodka and tonic arrives, and she clinks her glass against my beer. "Sure."

"Good."

***

I leave her in the motel bed before the sun is up. My skin is already ashy with more dust. Not black. Just barely a color you can see. Marissa—the sex worker—remarked last night about the sand on me. "How are you sandy? We're not anywhere near the beach."

"Work," was my reply, and then she got on her knees because she wanted those two crisp fifties I'd put on the nightstand.

The emerging sun is mottled by clouds. October is a good month to move. It's usually not too hot and not too cold. It might rain—quite frequently, actually—but that's okay, because the dust on my skin is less noticeable when I stand in the rain.

I have a duffle bag, a backpack full of books, my journal, and a small rubber duck Sister Mary gave me when I was little. I carry it to remind myself of her.

I get in my beat-to-shit car and head south.

I'm getting older, and I'm tired, so I figure one state away will do. I have a letter of recommendation from my boss that he gave me ages ago. I'd told him my mother was ill, and on the off chance that I had to go home, I'd love his recommendation.

He's a nice guy, so he did it, and left the date blank so I could fill it in later.

I cash my last check at Walmart because I don't have a bank account. There's no point.

The cycle is just beginning, so nothing really happens around me. If I don't stay in one place too long, I'll be fine.

I never do bad things. Bad things happen around me.

I'm almost to the Maryland state line when my cell phone rings. Not many people have the number. Just my current employer, a friend or two I might make along the way, and the orphanage.

When I see the number, my blood runs cold. There's only one reason they'd be calling me.

"Joe? It's Sister Frances."

There's a long pause as the nun waits for me to respond, but I can't unglue my tongue from the roof of my mouth. I finally manage, "Yes, Sister?"

"She's in a bad way, Joe. And she's asked for you. She worries. She's worried something bad has happened to you."

I let out a dark laugh and shake my head as the mile markers fly by, soft green blurs of radiating headlights in the dim October day. "Not to me, Sister F. *Around* me. I don't suffer. Others do."

"I understand, Joe." There's another pause before she says, "Well, to the best of my ability."

I'd always liked Sister Frances One, as the other nuns called her. She was a soft-spoken, brown-haired, blue-eyed nun who had a wicked sense of humor for a bride of God. Sister Frances Two was a bitter old battle axe who talked through gritted teeth when angry and laid into more than one ward with a wooden ruler.

"I know you do."

"But her health has taken a bad turn, Joe, and she's asking for you. Are you afraid to see her or—"

"I'm afraid to bring badness to the orphanage, Sister. I'm afraid of the darkness I carry."

"Let me do like the old days. We'll give you a nice, Godly bath—" she chuckles and I can't help but smile at her amusement. "We have plenty of Holy Water. In fact, with a priest on the grounds, we have an unlimited supply. You always meant so much to her. Will you consider it?"

I sigh. "I'm on my way," I say. "It will take me a while. I'm driving a piece of sh—crap car and it's not the speediest."

"Hurry, Joe. That's all I'll say."

"Yes, Sister." I disconnect the call.

I've just hit the Maryland state line. I now have a much longer way to go.

***

Somewhere in Virginia, I have to pull over. I need to eat. I need to sleep. My eyes feel full of sand, my head full of rocks, and my belly as barren as a desert.

I find a diner with a 24-hour sign glowing and another one that proclaims THE BEST PIE IN THE USA!

I doubt this, but I figure I'll give it a shot, anyway. Even a piece of mediocre pie, say 500th best in the USA, is fine with me.

When I enter, suddenly bathed in horrible fluorescent light, I see that my dust has already darkened. A little more visible now. As if I've been working in a cluttered attic or basement. I unroll my sleeves and button the cuffs. I can't do much about the dust that shows up on my face, but I do my best by keeping a scruff of a beard, my hair a bit longer, and wearing a cap often. It's the best I can do.

"How you doing, darlin'? Take a seat. Any one you want," the waitress says, waving her hand good-naturedly.

It's about two in the morning, and with the exception of an old couple in the corner, I'm the only patron.

"Coffee?"

I consider it and ask, "Is there a cheap motel around here anywhere? Unexpected road trip, and I am pooped. I'd love to sleep a while."

"About a half hour up the road. An old mom and pop place. Hell, I don't even think they have that Wi-Fi stuff like we do, but if you're just looking for a bed, that's a good, clean, and cheap place."

I smile at her. "Sold. I will take coffee, though. And I guess breakfast? It's the middle of the night—or way early in the morning, depending on how you look at it. My stomach is confused about what to eat."

"Whatever it wants," she says, then cackles. "We have breakfast, lunch, dinner, and dessert twenty four-seven."

She brings out my coffee along with a metal bowl full of creamers. Her name tag reads Doreen.

"Busy, tonight?" I ask, glancing at the menu.

She looks at the old folks. "That's Sal and Margie. They don't sleep well. They come in to shoot the shit on their particularly bad nights."

Margie's doing a crossword while Sal thumbs through a newspaper. They both have coffee steaming in front of them.

I have a flash of jealousy. To be in a relationship that long. To sit together and be silent and do whatever while just *being* together. I will never have that. I'll never put someone in harm's way by loving them.

I order the Early Bird Breakfast Bonanza: two eggs cooked to order, bacon, hash browns, sausage, a toasted English Muffin, and a side of fruit just for show. I'm on my second cup of coffee when Doreen brings it by.

She slams it down and rolls her eyes. She shakes her head, her soft mouth now pulled taut. In the corner, the old couple are bickering. Loudly.

"Not like them," she says. "Sorry if it's bothering you."

Ironically, I don't notice until she mentions it. I have no doubt the bickering is due to me. Nothing I can do. I'll eat and leave. Bars are the easiest to be in. Most of the time, alcohol dulls the effects of my presence. Sometimes, sadly, it exacerbates it.

"I'm fine. If you don't mind a refill and the check, I can eat and pay and get out of your hair."

In the corner, Margie yells something about an "Awl!" and Sal shakes his head like she's a fool.

Doreen gives me a curt nod and goes to get the coffeepot. I start eating my enormous breakfast. Coffee or no coffee, I'm so tired, and soon to be so full that it shouldn't be too hard to hit the bed and grab a few hours of sleep at this mom-and-pop motel she mentioned.

I study the back of my left hand as I eat. The dust is even darker now. Almost like silt on my skin.

I never feel bad. In fact, I feel like a good man. Which is why, on more than one occasion, I've considered washing down a big bottle of pills with an equally big bottle of Vodka. I just can't bring myself to do it. I'm a coward.

I'm handing Doreen my check and a ten-dollar bill for a seven-dollar tab when the inevitable blow is struck. It cracks like someone stepped on a dry branch in a silent forest. Doreen's head whips around, but I'm already facing the couple. Margie's holding her cheek and crying. Sal's looking at his hand as if he's never seen it before.

Doreen shakes her head, lowers her voice, conspiratorially. "It's been ages since he's done anything like that. Margie said not since he was drinking. And he stopped drinking twenty years ago. That's why she stayed with him."

I rise, knowing the sooner I leave, the better. "Keep the change," I say.

The door swings shut behind me just as I hear her yelling for Frank, no doubt the cook, who I imagine being a big burly guy used to slinging hash and dealing with late night problems with unruly people. Poor Sal. Poor Margie.

Sister Mary said God had made me. That there had to be a reason. I told her either God had fucked up, or maybe, just maybe, it wasn't God who'd made me at all.

I shake my head, then find my car and drive on down the road until I see a neon VACANCY sign. I get into my room and fall into bed, asleep before I even remember to feel guilty about the happenings of the day.

***

I wake up expecting to be in my old bed. Instead, I've drooled onto a pillow that who knows how many people before me have drooled on.

I shake my head to clear it and wish for more coffee. Maybe back to the diner? The food had been good, but it probably wasn't a great idea. I'd affected those folks enough.

I take a quick shower, brush my teeth, double check that I have my wallet, money, duffel bag, and haven't left anything behind.

Outside, the lady owner wheels a cleaning cart down the sidewalk in front of the units. Fresh out of the shower, the dust is still present.

"Didn't want to shower?" she asks, looking at my arms with a barely suppressed look of disgust.

"I did," I say. "Guess not well enough."

She cocks an eyebrow. "Want to go back in? I can skip your room and come back."

"No, ma'am. I'm fine. I have a dirty day ahead. I just have a pre-start."

That amuses her. "Don't forget there's complementary coffee in the office when you turn your key in."

"Ah, you're a godsend. I was just craving coffee. I like it good and strong."

"Well, you're in luck, because Luther—that's my husband—says mine will strip the paint off the walls."

"Perfect."

I say my goodbyes and hurry to the office. Luther is sitting behind the counter, holding an ice pack to his upper lip. My stomach falls. Already? So soon? Is the cycle accelerating? It happens sometimes, and there's nothing I can do. And other times, it slows way down. Almost as if in hibernation.

I wish this is one of those things I could predict. It isn't. And I've grown accustomed to it.

I make a huge cup of coffee and blow on it before taking a sip, but burn the shit out of my mouth anyway.

Luther eyes me and mumbles something.

"Sorry?"

"I said, take one for the road if you want. You can have more than one. You look pretty tired."

This is my opening. "Much obliged. Is everything okay? Did you hurt yourself?"

He chuckles and shakes his head, but the look in his eyes is far from amused. "The missus. She hit me right upside the head with her coffee cup. Because I told her she was in the way of the TV. She used to do stuff like that when she was a young firecracker. Then we'd work it out in the bedroom, if you know what I mean. But we're old now, so I wasn't expecting it."

I swallow a sigh. "Sorry to hear that."

He waves a liver-spotted hand and chuckles again. This time, it sounds genuine and not forced. "She'll get over it."

I nod. Because she will. Once I leave.

I doctor a second cup of very good, strong coffee and nod. "Take care of that lip, sir."

"Will do. Be careful on the road, boy. And no offense—"

I wait, knowing what's coming.

"You could use a shower, son."

"Yes, sir." I get in my car, put both cups of coffee in the cup holders, and crank up Elton John's *Bennie and the Jets* on the oldies station. Getting on the road is the best I can do. I'm not going to get any cleaner.

The goal today is to get through a good bit of Tennessee. I'm grateful, given I'm headed south, that it's October. October won't be too terrible. I won't sweat incessantly. What makes black dust more obvious? Sweat. It creates rivers of gray sludge on my skin. Not easy to disguise, if you ask me.

I drink my coffee, wondering why the process has sped up. Is it possible that it's due to Sister Mary's failing health? She's always been my champion. The closest thing to a mother I've ever had in my unfortunate, filthy life.

I crank up the music when I get tired of thinking. I wish I still smoked, consider starting again, and then shake my head. I'm already ash-colored on the outside often enough. No need to be that way on the inside, too. I don't necessarily want to die, but I don't necessarily want to live, either.

I focus on my single night with that sweet female companion and let those memories occupy my thoughts instead of the ones that might otherwise go dark.

Sister Mary had started with pain a few years back, which escalated. Breast cancer. Then a double mastectomy with her refusing reconstructive surgery. We'd talked on the phone afterwards, and she'd said, "Joe, God doesn't care if I have a banging rack, so why should I?" I had laughed so hard I'd cried. When I'd disconnected, I'd simply cried. With relief, mostly, that I hadn't lost her yet.

I never get to see her, but the world is still a better place with her in it. No one can convince me otherwise.

My piece of shit car chews up the miles while my mind jumps around the timeline of my life. Sister Mary had told me, and Sister Frances One had confirmed, that I'd arrived on the doorstep in a dirty box with a dirty blanket. Of course, they'd been appalled, thinking I'd been abused and kept in deplorable conditions. They'd cleaned me well, diapered me, swaddled me in new clothing, and put me in a much used but still spic-and-span crib.

Hours later, they'd conferred on exactly why the new baby was dusty again.

"It was amazing," she'd said. "We all stared at one another, almost accusingly. I mean, someone must have handled this baby and gotten him dirty."

"What did you do?" I'd asked.

"We gave you another bath, new diaper, new clothes, new bedding on the crib, wiped down the crib. Then we all sat there, Joe, five of us, like we were watching a movie. We watched you be a baby. And then we watched the dust appear, collect, and darken."

"Why didn't you all turn on each other? Why doesn't what I am affect you or the other kids?"

She had smiled at me.

"That is what I'm trying to tell you." She'd pointed a bony finger toward the ceiling, but not really; she pointed through the ceiling, into the sky, above the sky, to the heavens. To Heaven with a capital H. "I think we can protect you at the orphanage with our collected blessings from Him."

"Not convinced, Sister. I just think that the holiness and the perceived sanctity of the place cancels out the badness I carry around."

"But you are not bad, Joe," she'd stressed, taking my hand.

"If you say so, Sister."

Somewhere in Chastain, Tennessee, I get hungry. I don't want to go in and eat, but I have to eat. I find a McDonald's and go through the drive thru.

As I exit, a bag of hot food in my lap, I see the two cars that were ahead of me have pulled to the side to have a vehement argument. The man throws his food, the woman waves her bony finger. Both faces are angry, spittle flying, voices raised.

I'm just happy they aren't fist fighting each other.

"Definitely an accelerated cycle," I say, brushing dust off my forearm onto my pants. When I glance back at my arm after eating a few fries, it was like I'd never wiped it off.

I drive until my eyelids are heavy. I drive until I know pulling over is my only option. If I keep driving, I'll either hit and kill someone or kill myself. I pull over in a parking lot behind a Walmart, get out, pee in a bush, get in the back seat, and curl up to sleep. I want to minimize my contact with other people for as long as possible.

Somewhere around dawn, there's a tapping on the window. I look up and stifle a groan. It's a cop. This is bad.

I put on a fake smile, nod, and raise a finger as I slide along the back seat to pop the door latch. My car is an old hatchback, so I can't reach the handle to roll my window down. "Sorry, officer. I can't reach—"

"No sleeping here," he says brusquely.

"I'm sorry. I was nodding off on the road. Thought it was safer to—"

"Some of these stores don't mind if big rigs and the like pull in for the night. This one, however, has a sign posted: no overnight parking. You'll have to move along, sir."

I nod. "Will do, officer. Sorry."

He studies me carefully, as if scanning for an infraction that would allow him to give me a more justified once over. He apparently doesn't find anything.

"There's a truck stop a ways up," he says. His eyes are blue. Cold. But his demeanor has softened slightly. "Has showers and the like. And they don't care if you take a snooze in the parking lot."

I glance down to see that I am not just dusty. I am grimy.

I don't think I've ever been this grimy.

My phone rings and I glance at it. It's the orphanage, but I don't want to piss off a cop who's clearly trying to be nice. The man could be giving me a ticket, or worse, but he's not. So, I let the phone ring, hoping against hope that it's not bad news about Sister Mary.

"I think that's a great idea, officer. I know the one you mean. Now that I'm not falling asleep behind the wheel, I can drive up there and catch a shower, some coffee, and maybe another cat nap."

He backs up and waves me out. I climb out and stretch, then adjust my seat. I don't offer to shake his hand, and he seems relieved. "Thank you, sir," I manage.

My heart is hammering. I just want him to leave so I can take a deep breath and call the orphanage back. He seems to be debating. He makes a decision, tips his hat, and says, "Be careful out there."

Then he returns to his car, saying something into the squawking radio on his shoulder. When he opens the door, the interior light comes on, and I see that there is no one in the back of his squad car. Relief floods me.

I let my heart settle and then climb into the car. I find the recent call in my phone and hit the RETURN CALL button.

"Sister Frances?" I ask when it's answered.

"No, son. It's me."

I pause, heart in my throat. But at least that answers one question. She isn't dead. She's on the phone.

"Sister, what's wrong? Everything okay?"

"Besides dying, I'm fine," she says and cackles.

She always did have a warped sense of humor for a nun. Or maybe *because* she's a nun.

"Sister..."

"On the off chance that my cancer beats you, I want you to know that your illness is my fault, and I have left you a plot of land in Montana."

"So, how much medication *do* they have you on?" I attempt to joke.

"Enough morphine to fell an elephant. And unfortunately, it isn't doing shit, pardon my French. I am immune to that sweet relief at this point. It's spread and metastasized—the cancer, I mean. At this point, it's just a waiting game, and all the drugs do is keep the edge off so I don't scream."

I shut my eyes and will myself not to get emotional. I fail. My throat grows tight, my eyes prick with tears, and I simply wait for her to talk.

"Did you hear me, Joseph? Your condition is my fault."

I shake my head. "That can't be. I was left there."

"True. But I had...*prayed* for you. And then there you were."

She hesitated on prayed and I wonder why, but I let it go. We can leave that bit for when we come face-to-face. And if that doesn't come, well, that's fine. Because I am pretty damn sure that Sister Mary is high as a kite, despite her protestations.

"Sister—"

"Joseph, just listen. The Readers' Digest Condensed version: I prayed for you. To release me and the other sisters from some of our sins. Things that had led us to the convent. To change our lives. Your affliction is due to that. I will explain more when you're here—"

"I'll get there sooner if you let me off the—"

"Hush!"

My mouth snaps closed so fast that my teeth click. Old habits die hard.

"The other thing is, I've willed you a plot of land. The papers are in my wardrobe in my last worldly outfit. You'll recognize them because they are *jeans*, Joseph. Can you imagine me in jeans?"

"No, Sister." I laugh, and she does, too.

"Now get off the phone and hurry up."

"Yes, Sister. Oh, and Sister?"

"Yes?"

"The cycle this time..." I realize I've lowered my voice as if someone else can hear me. "It's faster."

"It's because I'm dying," she says. "My prayer is that when I die, you are released. But I don't think that's the case. I think we all have to be dead. All I know is, I'm sorry. I'm sorry that you're paying for our sins." With that, she hangs up.

I look at my phone and shake my head. I have no idea what to make of that. So, I won't think about anything. I'll just drive and then drive some more.

I find a deserted drive-thru and order two large coffees, a greasy breakfast sandwich, and a handheld hash brown thing. I eat the food way too fast and then sip my coffee way too slow. There's a porta potty near some construction materials in the parking lot. I duck in, use the odoriferous facilities, and douse my hands in hand sanitizer. Then it's back on the road. All accomplished with minimal human interaction.

Arkansas is a struggle. I'm bored. I'm worried. And I keep replaying my bizarre conversation with Sister Mary in my head.

I'm determined to make it to her by the following day. I feel even that's pushing it. My inner clock is tick-tick-ticking. My worst fear is that I'll arrive too late and never know what the hell she meant. Never understand why she blames herself or why she's left me land I didn't know about. As far as my understanding goes, that land should go to the orphanage. It isn't a contract, per se, but it was expected of the sisters to give up all worldly possessions, as anything of value went to God. Not an orphan like me.

I find the most deserted diner I can at eleven at night. I pull on a hoodie and a cap and shove my hands into the kangaroo pocket. I keep my head down as I order from Darla, my overly friendly waitress. Burger, fries, pie, and a cup of coffee (keep it coming).

"You got it, hon," she says and saunters off. Her yellow uniform is a bit too tight, but even well into her forties, she pulls it off. She has a nice figure and knows how to swing that back porch.

I'm starving, and from the looks of it, I'm the only one here besides her and the cook. Thank goodness greasy spoons still exist in the day and age of twenty-four-hour fast food and mega convenience stores. Both are great if you can be around people without them turning on each other. Me, not so much.

My meal doesn't take long because I asked for my burger medium. She slides my plate across the table and refills my coffee. I forget myself for a moment and pull my hands free of my sweatshirt while she stands there. Dust sifts down off my hands, onto my burger, onto the table. I grit my teeth as she gasps.

"Oh, my gosh. I can get you—"

I laugh, put my hands back in the pockets. "It's fine. My kids—always playing practical jokes. A pocket full of dust." I shake my head, feigning amusement.

"Oh, hon. I can get you another—"

She reaches for it and I am so fucking tired. So very done with this. With life. With being me. "No, leave it!" I say a bit too gruffly.

She freezes, nods, and says slowly, "Okaaaaay." Then she leaves me. "Jesus Christ," I hear her mutter under her breath as she goes.

I've never seen it like this. I am reminded of Pigpen in the Charlie Brown comics. I am Pigpen. I am dirty. I am an unclean soul. That is what I think, what I've always thought. But according to the only person I've ever viewed as a parent, it isn't my fault. It is hers.

I eat my food, throw fifteen bucks down for an eleven-dollar check, and use the restroom. I wash my hands vigorously, watching brackish gray water swirl down the drain. I dry my hands on a paper towel, throw it out, and exit into the cool October night.

When I turn the key in the ignition, my hands are already black again.

***

"Joe!" Sister Frances One answers the door. She grabs me in her arms despite my filth. She isn't in a habit. Oh, how times have changed. She's wearing a pair of sensible blue slacks and moccasins. A light cardigan is draped around her skinny shoulders. She has aged like so many women do, becoming smaller, bird-like. A miniature version of their former youthful selves. Her smile is still contagious, and I find myself smiling back.

"How are you?" she asks, patting me. She utterly ignores the puff of dust that comes up from my jacket like she's beating a dirty old sofa.

"I'm dirty. I need to be doused, I guess. Like the old days."

She nods. "Do you want to do it now? We can make a trip into the baptismal bath. We haven't used it in years, to be honest, but it worked just fine the last time we checked. The bath itself is blessed by Father McMahon, so anything that comes from the pipes is Holy Water. Or we can go into the church proper and I can dump a bucket of blessed water straight over you like when you were young and incorrigible."

I look around, remembering how, at certain stages of my cycle, the nuns periodically had to remove me from the other children. The sanctuary of the church and hallowed ground helped, but didn't rule out fights among the other kids.

I was often alone, with only nuns as company. Still, life could have been worse.

"Should I talk to her first?" I ask, lassoing my wandering attention.

"It's up to you. She's sleeping, but she rouses easily and welcomes visitors and distractions."

"Is she on a ridiculous number of drugs, Sister? Because she was saying some crazy stuff on the phone."

Sister Frances looks surprised. "She called you?"

"Yes, yesterday. I think it was yesterday." I shake my head. I'm tired to my bones. "Arkansas and Texas somehow blurred together. I've been driving as much as possible. And—" I shake my hands before her and we both watch the dirt fall off me, "—minimizing contact with other people."

"Oh, Joe," she says. She shakes her head. "She's on a lot of morphine, but it's doing its job, and she has quite a tolerance. A dose from that pump that would kill you or me, leaves her almost pain free, but not quite. And, to be honest, sharp as the proverbial tack."

"Interesting."

"Do you want to sleep first?" she asks.

It's only then that I realize I'm yawning hugely. "No. It's fine. I've gone longer than this without sleep. I want to see her, but I'm not sure about letting her see how rapidly this thing is going. This fresh cycle started the night before you called me."

"Let's see what happens," she says. I follow her back to the rear of the building towards the baptismal font. It's not some wussy pedestal with a bowl full of water. It's a big concrete bath, in which an adult sized person can be fully immersed. All around it are elaborate mosaic murals of biblical scenes. I haven't been in it since my own group baptism as a child. The nuns never knew if a child had been baptized, so they played it safe and assumed they hadn't. We'd walked through like an assembly line in our white linen gowns as Father Davis had blessed each and every one of us.

She turns the faucet, and the old pipe groans. She chuckles. "I promise you, we run it regularly to keep it operational. No need to worry."

I shake my head; groaning pipes or possible stagnant water are the least of my worries. "It's fine, Sister."

"So, how's life been?" she asks, looking as if she fears the answer.

"Lonely," I say.

She bows her head, and I see her eyes are shiny with unshed tears. I feel bad for that, but my life is a constant game of hiding myself. It's nice to talk to someone who knows about me. Even if it's a sad fucking state of affairs.

We watch the tub fill up in silence. It's a companionable silence, so I appreciate it.

"You can go in nude or clothed. It doesn't matter," she says as the water approaches halfway up the concrete wall.

"How about skivvies, Sister? I don't want to offend your sensibilities."

She snorts, and I smile. "Do you know how many boys I've raised, Joe?"

"No."

"Me either," she says. "I've lost count. The point is, seeing you in the altogether isn't going to scar me for whatever little life I have left. I might be a nun, but I have seen a penis."

There's a twinkle in her eyes, so I can't resist saying, "You naughty old bird."

This makes her laugh outright, which makes it that much easier to whisk all my clothes off and step up onto the side of the baptismal font, only to take two steps down into it. There is no priest present to dunk me or cup the water over my head. To say a prayer over me, ask for a cleansing of my soul, or reassure me that my life is not useless, wasted, or the one that is my worst fear deep down inside me where the truth lives—evil.

The water is tepid at best. But it's not so cold outside yet that I'm chilled down to the bone. So far, this fall has none of that raw rainy weather that makes the insides of my knees and elbows ache. Still, I shiver.

"I should have waited to make it warmer, but you know, there's not much temperature control. It's meant to be brief." She smiles.

"It's fine. I have a feeling I could soak in here for hours, Sister, and still come out as dirty as the inside of a coal miner's asshole."

"Joseph!" But we both laugh as we watch the scum of dirt settle atop the formerly clean water. My skin is letting go of its load, but I have a feeling it won't last for long.

Something tells me the moment I climb from God's Whirlpool, I'm going to be as grimy as ever. In that case,

I guess it's best that I'm here at the convent, where I am known and loved anyway. The nuns aren't scared of my weird affliction. They don't shun me for something I can't control.

I lower myself all the way and sink under, letting the water close in over my neck, then my head, and then my face. The world is dulled, muffled, invisible but for the shimmery, blurry outlines above the water. I've considered drowning myself before. Tying big cinder blocks around my ankles and jumping into a dam. I've also considered pills, and gassing myself. Just feeding the hose from my tailpipe into my piece of shit car. Most likely, no one would bother checking my shack on the border of the quarry's property for quite a while. It would probably be ages before anyone discovered me, a dead man covered in black dust. I gave drinking myself to death a shot once or twice, but I'd only ended up sick as a dog with no memory of anything and no friends to report back to me what I'd done.

I see Sister Frances standing over me. I've been underwater for a while. Holding my breath. Thinking. Part of me wants to curl up at the foot of Sister Mary's bed like her pet dog and die with her. Part of me wants to run.

The orphanage is home, but it's also my history and my roots. Those things can be uncomfortable.

I hear my name, garbled by the barrier of water. "Joe? Are you okay, Joe?"

I consider opening my mouth, drinking in the now-soiled water. Instead, I sit up and take a deep breath. "As good as I'm going to get, Sister."

***

It's coming back even as I'm getting dressed. Sister sees it too, because she sighs.

"It's fine," I say.

"It isn't. You deserve better than this."

I cock an eyebrow at her. I think she knows what Sister Mary had in mind when she called. "Do you know what's going on here, Sister?"

She looks, for the first time that I can ever recall, uncertain and guarded. "I think I know what's on her mind. But it's not my place to say. Though I played a part in it, I guess. So did Sister Frances—"

"Two," I interject.

"Yes. And Sister Theodore."

"Is she still alive?" I ask, smiling. Sister Theodore always reminded me of the Chipmunk with the same name. Plump, cute, soft-spoken, and a little skittish.

"We all are but for Frances Two. She fell ill a few years back and passed on about a year ago. Colon cancer."

"I'm sorry to hear that, Sister."

She nods and sighs. "Let's go see if she's awake. No offense, but she would kick my ass—pardon my French, my Lord—if I told you the stuff she felt it was her obligation to tell you. And Mary takes the bulk of the responsibility as hers. Every time I look in there when she happens to be awake, she's doing her penance."

I can picture her; I've seen her doing it. Eyes shut, head bowed, mouth moving but very little sound coming out. Or holding her rosary, saying the prayer diligently, "Hail Mary, full of grace, the Lord is with thee..."

I'm not religious by any stretch, but I can break out with any prayer, word for word, you might throw at me.

I hate to think of her feeling guilty. I hate to think of her doing penance to excess. I hate to think of her dying, if I'm honest.

"Let's go," Sister Frances says, taking my hand with her thin, cool fingers. Her skin feels like the finest, thinnest leather. Softer than soft. "If she dies while we're standing here speculating, she'll haunt us for all eternity."

That makes me bark nervous laughter, and together we go through the chilly, echoing halls of the orphanage. There are no young children here anymore. The nuns have aged too much. The higher ups saw fit to make it a half-way house for troubled or homeless teens. Less physical work, more spiritual. Job-building skills, home economics, curfews, and support meetings.

The chill in the halls reminds me of childhood. Mysterious dust and conflicts. A family made almost solely of women dressed like penguins.

I'm surprised to feel my eyes prick with tears. I'm going to see the closest thing I've ever had to a mother, and she's dying.

Sister knocks with a light touch, and I smile. It's barely audible. There's no answer, and my heart drops, my stomach twists, my hands take up a fine tremor. Are we too late?

Sister knocks again, harder this time, and I hear it. It's whispery and fine and super soft like Sister Frances's aged skin—

"Come in."

We enter, and Sister Mary smiles. "There's my boy. I am so sorry for my sins against you," she says and surprises us both by bursting into tears.

Sister Frances pats my hand and then turns and leaves.

I'm alone with Sister Mary, and I have no idea what to do or say.

"Don't cry, Sister..." It's the best I can do.

***

She has one of the teens bring us a tray of tea and cookies. "I won't eat much," she says. "But you should. You should eat and drink. I can enjoy it by watching you."

I shake my head. She's so thin. Her eyes are shiny from the drugs, but despite the sheen, they are still as clear as can be. Sane, alert, aware.

I take a cookie, the kind with the blob of hardened red jelly in the middle. Those have always been my favorite, and she must have remembered because there are more of those than any other kind. My second favorite are also present and numerous: the butter cookies that look like little pretzels covered in chunky sugar to resemble salt.

I eat my cookie, red blob first, while she busies herself with her shaking hands. "Do you still take two sugars and cream, Joseph?"

I used to sit and have tea with the nuns when I felt too alone. I nod, even though I now take one sugar instead of two. I'm no kid anymore.

She makes it perfectly and hands me the mug. They're painted milk glass. The same mugs the orphanage has had forever. I sip my tea and it tastes like home.

"I prayed for you," she says, launching right in. I keep my mouth shut, parting my lips only to sip my tea.

"I felt—we felt, all of us—that we were too dark to be nuns. To be here for children. We were the church's problem children." She smiles wryly, and something in me perks to life. It feels like fear. Mild, but unpleasant.

I keep my mouth shut and wait. I want her to talk. She always told me it was better to listen more and talk less. It's not an easy lesson to learn, but I feel like over the years, I've gotten a handle on it.

"I have been given permission by the other Sisters to tell you the full story. Not Sister Frances Peterson, of course. She's dead. So why keep the secret of a dead woman, am I right?" Another wry smile and she keeps going as if she fears slowing down will keep the story buried.

"Sister Frances One—Roberts, I mean, who I know you love, was an abused wife. Her husband beat her terribly—" She shakes her head and looks away as if the thought of someone beating Sister Frances is unbearable. To me, it certainly is. "She retaliated. She didn't kill him, mind you, but she put him in a coma."

I blink. I wasn't expecting this part. "But certainly—"

She raises her hand, and I shut my mouth. "He deserved it?"

I nod, realizing I'd learn much more if I kept my promise to myself to keep my mouth shut.

"I'm sure he did. She's not the kind of woman to retaliate physically for any reason. So, if she did, it was a damn good reason. She hit him with an iron. An old-fashioned one made from actual cast iron. He was in a coma when she came here. To our knowledge, he never woke up. And I say good for her," she says softly. Then she kisses her cross necklace as if in penance. "Luckily, she had a friend in the clergy who was able to pull some strings. Get her an annulment order. Otherwise, she wouldn't have been able to become a nun, as you know."

I shrug. I hadn't remembered, but that's okay.

"Let's talk about Sister Frances Two," she starts, and I realize I'm holding my breath. "She was raised in a very strict Catholic family. Which doesn't sound that traumatic, does it?"

I shake my head and pick up a pretzel cookie. I have forgotten how good these things are. Makes me feel like a kid again. There's a certain kind of peace and comfort to it. Feelings I haven't felt in a very long time.

She gives me a succinct nod. "When I say strict, I mean it. Penance for simply existing. Floggings for anything her father saw as insubordination or a sin. He took liberties as well."

I swallow hard. This is all news to me. Somehow, growing up, my mind told me that since the Sisters were following their passion—doing God's work—life must have been easy for them. Cake.

Not so much.

"He never fully…" She clears her throat, shakes her head, and for the first time hits the bolus button on the morphine pump. It hisses softly, and almost immediately her eyes seem glazed. Dreamy. But her expression never softens and she goes on. "He never penetrated her. The sex act, I mean, as it's defined, didn't take place. But there was fondling and penetration in other ways, and of course…" She blanches, and I want to tell her she doesn't have to say it. I get the picture. And I feel bad for every time I'd called Frances Two an old battle axe growing up. "Oral penetration," she finishes.

I exhale softly. I am no longer interested in eating the cookies.

"The problem with that, beyond the obvious," she goes on, "is that he not only did that to her, but then he also punished her sin. The sin *she* committed with her father. He punished her for being desirable to him. He beat her. And he broke her mentally. She was in quite a state when she got here, and it was only daily prayer and therapy and the priests who came and rallied around her that got her to the mental place she was when you children met her. But she was wickedly smart and could, at times, be wonderfully funny. I often wonder what Frances would have been like without her father's curse on her."

My chest aches.

Sister Mary clears her throat. Her eyes are shiny but alert. "Right. I'm very sorry to be putting you through hearing all this, Joseph."

I shrug. "It's fine. You do whatever you need to, Sister."

"I would very much like to tell you the story so you will understand."

"Go on," I say. I pat her thin, frail hand, and she smiles.

"Theodore, well, she had her own tales of woe. She fell in love with a boy. And she got pregnant. Now, we all know what we're *supposed* to say in that situation, but I have always felt that even if the child is a product of two people's inability to save themselves for marriage, then so be it. I do not think God turns his back on children conceived or born out of wedlock. A child is a child. Innocent. A lamb of God. His or her parents 'mistake'—" She does air quotes, and I smile, "—isn't the child's fault. And who really cares how they get here? When they are here on Earth, they are a clean soul and might go on to do many bold and wonderful things."

"This is why you were born to do this job, Sister," I laugh.

She rolls her eyes but gives me a smile. Then her face sobers.

"Sadly, not everyone agrees with my forward way of thinking. Theodore's boyfriend didn't. He beat her. He beat her into a miscarriage. It crushed her. She blamed herself. She thought if only she had been stronger. If only she had fought back. Several months later…" Sister Mary stops and I wait.

I wait until the crawling sense of anxiety fills my chest and I cave. "What happened, Sister?" I prompt as gently as possible. My right leg is moving like a jackhammer, bouncing up and down. Nervous habit. Dust sifts down from the bare skin between my pant leg and sock, leaving what looks like a small pile of human cremains.

"She killed him," she says. "She told us. She injected him with some of her father's insulin. Her father was diabetic. Her boyfriend was not. She waited until he fell asleep in front of a movie and injected him and let him die."

These nuns are turning out to be spitfires. My brain offers up that odd thought, and I have to suppress a laugh.

"And you?" I ask.

"Saved the best for last," she says with a sigh. She hits her bolus, and I put my hand on her hand.

"Sister, we can do this another day if you're too tired. We don't have to—"

"I might not have another day, Joseph. I don't know. But I can't take the chance. We all had this giant confession one night as the orphanage was being set up. We had some wine."

I raise an eyebrow.

"Oh, nuns drink. Some too much, if you get me. And so do priests. And I never said this, but priests drink very *often* and too much. We were all getting to know each other, as it were. It was Theodore who cracked first. She's such a character. She reminds me of—"

"Theodore the Chipmunk," I blurt.

She smiles. "Yes. Bingo. Funny, isn't it?"

"It is." I hand her her tea, and she takes it with shaking fingers. "Tell me, Sister. Then you can rest."

Her eyes tear up and she says, "Oh, Joseph. I'm so very sorry."

I shake my head and pat her hand. "Just tell me."

"When I was young, my uncle molested me. Not molested—" She shakes her head. "That's such a nice name for such an awful thing. It somehow softens it, when that should never happen. He raped me. Over and over again. He lived with my mother and myself. He had nowhere else to live, so she let him move in. She was a single mom. The money helped, and I think that the presence of a man—a protector—in the house was nice to her. But it wasn't, to me."

My stomach is in knots. Every one of these women who dedicated their lives to children without homes or loved ones or caring parents went through the wringer. They all have such grotesque, ugly histories that it would be so much easier to just look away.

"I'm sorry, Sister. There's not much anyone can say but that, is there?"

She shakes her head, and this time, she pats my hand in consolation.

"Finally, one day, I told my mother. I was shaking when I did. My stomach was so upset, I nearly threw up. I had to stop and start about three times. At one point, I gagged. But I told her everything. The visits in the night. The pain. The torture. At one point, I hesitated to call it torture. But then I realized that was probably the most accurate description of all." She starts to weep silently, and my heart cracks in half.

I wait and let her get it out. Tears can be cleansing. I know this as well as anyone.

Finally, she takes a deep breath and says, "She knew."

My brain hurts as I hear those words. "She knew?"

"She told me he'd done the same to her as a young girl. But it was such a small price to pay for the help with money and the house, didn't I agree? And she finished with, 'And you get used to it after a while, honey. It's not that big a deal.' I was bleeding from the night before as she said that, Joe. And I hated her. A rage like I had never felt filled me up. Black and strong and bitter, like poison."

I hold my breath. This is the important part. This is the meat of the story. This is where the whole thing comes together.

She hits the bolus again and it beeps. "Damn it. I'm trying too soon. Maybe just because I'm nervous to say it out loud. Morphine makes you brave." She winks at me.

"I burned down the house," she says quickly. "I burned it down with both of them inside. It burned and raged and consumed until there was very little left but black dust and ash."

My gaze goes to the pile at my feet. My own cruddy skin. And I feel my heart sink. What does this mean?

"Sister—"

She waves a hand at me and I go silent.

"Now I'm going to finish. You're going to stay quiet like the old days when you were all too rambunctious and I had silent time. Do you understand, Joe?"

I nod, showing her I still know how to play the game.

"When we arrived here, we all had a long chat one night over many glasses of overly fruity wine. That's how women get a bad name. They drink stuff that tastes like liquid candy when they should drink the good stuff." She winks at me again and I smile. Sister Mary is downplaying what she's about to say with jokes. "We all told our sordid tales. Of course, mine was the most horrific. I am, in fact, a double murderer."

My heart quickens to hear her say that. I could never think of her that way. Even after that confession.

"I was worried. It ate at me a lot, but I'd been doing a stellar job of stuffing it down. I was good at stuffing things down—until I snapped and I couldn't any longer. I went to bed that night, after hearing their stories, thinking we were the most rag-tag, ill-fitted women to be caring for young children without anyone else in the world. I felt we were too dirty. Too unclean. Me, most of all."

She takes a deep breath and studies her nails. She looks like she might cry again. I hope she doesn't, because then I might cry, too.

"I was sad and had insomnia and I had to move, to do something. I took the remainder of that atrocious bottle of rotten grape juice and wandered down in the archives. This used to be a monastery. It was converted when the church needed a building for the orphanage.

They'd moved the monks to another location. There was a ton of storage down there that they'd used to shove old files and papers and...books."

The hair on the back of my neck stands up at the final word. The way she said it tells me that my fate had been sealed—or created—by one of those books.

"I found it in a small section low to the ground, far back in the stacks. I was simply wandering, understand me. But I was nosey. Always have been. It's been a blessing and a curse throughout my life. I have learned a lot. And also, I made a lot of mistakes. All thanks to my need to pry and poke and learn."

I keep my word and keep my mouth shut. I don't say a word. I simply wait. My heart thumps harder. I'm not quite sure why.

"It had no title. No markings. It was a red book with uneven pages. The ink inside was faded and it looked old. Very old. I flipped through it, and it almost seemed to open itself to the page marked, "*Mule: One who carries the burden of others. Marked by the ash and dirt of the world.*" It was a spell, I assume. Looked like nonsense to me, but something in my spine shivered when I read it. Some part of me woke up. Some part of me saw a chance. We could possibly be cleansed to serve the Lord and the children appropriately. Trust me, Joseph... I had no—if I'd had any idea..."

I shake my head. I just want to know at this point. I'm tired of wondering. I wave my hand in an encouraging manner.

"I brought it up to my room and slept with it on my bedside table for days before I approached the others. It was Sister Frances Two who wanted to burn the book. She said it felt *off*. I told her she was worried for no reason. Most likely, not one damn thing would happen. Good, bad, or otherwise. We'd just look like a bunch of fools. It was nonsense."

She levels her watery blue gaze at me, and her spidery fingers reach out to push the bolus. The machine hisses and her body's tension relaxes.

"Even as I protested to them, telling them it was nonsense and just mumbo jumbo, I knew it was a lie. I knew it was something. I knew it would make me better. It just never occurred to me it would make anyone else worse."

She takes a deep breath. Continues. "The children weren't here yet, but they were coming. During another three wine bottle kind of night, I pulled out the book. Trying to play it off almost like one of those terrible horror movies where the sorority girls say a spell and unleash something horrible. And then there's ninety minutes of them trying to rectify it."

I smile at the reference. She's the only nun I know who likes horror movies.

"It rhymed. Terribly. The spelling was off. Definitely English, but as if it was written back in the days when people spelled things phonetically. Part of me felt its power, if I'm honest. Part of me thought it was a joke. Or at the very least, an 'it can't hurt to try' scenario." She gives me a wry smile. "You know, how some people view prayer."

I want a cigarette. I haven't smoked in years. I feel like we're approaching a part of the tale I don't want to hear.

"There we are, four nuns in our nightgowns, with wine stained lips. We recite this...spell, for lack of a better word. To call forth a mule. Which sounds like the least scary thing in the world. We want to be better people. Leave behind our sins and raise these needful children to be good, God-fearing humans. But instead, we saddled you with our sins."

I blink.

I'm the mule.

I mean, I already knew. But to hear her say it is hard.

"How do you know?"

She shuts her bright eyes and chuckles darkly. "You showed up a day later. Alone. No parents. No note. And the dust covering you. The ash. The darkness. Those were our sins. And they never left you. Occasionally, it would slow a bit with Holy Water, but rarely."

My hands are at war with themselves in my lap. I am the one who now bears the burden of two murders, several violent retaliations, and more. I am the one who gets to lug around their darkness. Their dirt.

But I can't bring myself to be mad.

"And the fights that break out around me? The bad things that happen?"

She looks like she wants to touch me, but doesn't. Not because I'm dirty, but because she's ashamed. "We think it's just because you carry around unadulterated sin. It's the very nature of sin, Joseph. It has a mark, it has a *feel* to it. One-on-one with someone, it can often be harmless. In a group, it can cause problems." She shrugs, cries harder. "But that's just a theory. We don't know for sure. We don't know *anything* for sure."

I take a deep breath to steady myself. "It is what it is, Sister."

She levels a finger at me and says, "I hate that bullshit saying. Just like I hate the whole 'God helps those who help themselves.' That one always did get under my skin."

I want to laugh, but this new knowledge has me feeling exhausted.

"We tried to reverse it, Joseph," she says. "I need you to know that. We went and we prayed. I searched the archives and that damn book for a reversal, a counter spell or something else that would fix it. Anything. We looked. We prayed. And it never worked. We all held that guilt all these years. We were devastated when you left. We wanted you to stay so we could care for you. Be your family, at least. Make some amends for the damage."

I look at her. "Do you think I was…created to take your sin? Do you think I was ever really a regular baby who was simply unwanted or couldn't be cared for, so I was dropped off? Or do you think the spell *created me*? Do I even have a soul, or am I simply the receptacle for all your perceived sins?"

She shakes her head, lips pressed tightly together. Her spidery fingers creep to the bolus and push it. "I do not know. I wish I knew. I wish I could say it's a coincidence, but it would be a hell of one, wouldn't it?"

I nod.

She clears her throat as if preparing to speak in public. "I have a piece of property I inherited from my aunt. She hated my uncle. He'd done the same to her as a child. She was ten years younger than him. She left me a bit of retirement land, as she put it. To keep or give to the church—whatever I saw fit. Technically, I should have turned it over to the church, but I sat on it, because I saw fit to give it to you, Joseph."

I shake my head. "You should give it to the church, Sister."

"No, I should give it to you. Something for yourself. A place you don't have to scrimp and save for. A place where you can be yourself. No hiding. No questions. No..." She lowers her voice. "Whores."

I laugh. She knows. "What? Does this house come with an in-house girlfriend?"

She rolls her eyes. "No. I guess getting...company is still valid and has to be your decision."

"Sister, I don't feel right taking it."

"Joe, I don't feel right if you don't."

I sigh.

"Do you want to deny a sick old woman her dying wish?"

This is the part where I'm supposed to tell her she's not dying, but she is. It's the truth.

"Of course not."

"Good." She reaches for the nightstand, but her hands falter. I go to her side and she points. There's a large accordion folder, and I get it for her.

I try to hand it to her, but she pushes it away. "That's yours. All the information from my lawyer. The deed to the land. Information about the house. Contact information for the family that act as caretakers—and by that, I mean clean it three times a year and try to keep vermin out." She winks. "No promises on that vermin thing."

Then she levels her gaze at me carefully and says, "Everything you need is in there, Joe. Please take it, and please have the happiest life you can manage. I worry about you. And I will die with the knowledge that any hardships you've had in this life are due to me and my stupidity."

"You're not stupid, Sister. You wanted to be better. Your intentions were good." I put my hand on hers. Her skin is tissue paper thin, soft, and cold. Her fingers tremble beneath my palm.

"You know what they say, Joe." Her eyes seem to bore into me, and she looks like she's terrified.

"What?"

"The road to Hell is paved with good intentions. And I am almost certain I'm going to see it for myself very soon."

My stomach rolls. The thought of her going to Hell hurts me. I don't believe in it, per se. The nuns showed me love and laughter and humor and family, but the religion thing never stuck. But Sister Mary believes in it and must be terrified. That is what upsets me.

"You're not going to Hell," I tell her.

"From your lips…" she says softly and smiles. She pats my hand. "Go on, then. I'm very tired and very full of drugs. Let Frances make you something to eat. She always was the best cook of us all and has done nothing but improve even more since you left."

"Then she must be magical now," I say.

"She is."

"I'll come see you in a bit."

"Yes, do that. I missed you," she says, her eyelids drifting shut.

"I missed you, too, Sister."

***

When I return hours later, she's staring at the ceiling. But she no longer sees it. Her skin is just starting to cool. Her body looks even smaller than it was during her confession to me. Death shrinks a person. As if when the soul leaves, the body deflates. A husk. The thought turns my blood cold, and I turn away quickly. I want to remember her bright eyes and her jokes, not this.

I take Sister Frances up on staying at the convent for only a few days. I help her with arrangements and contacting the Archdiocese about bringing in a new nun since it's down to just her and sweet Theodore.

I can't help but look at them all differently now. Knowing their secrets. The sins they wished to put on the mule's back.

She doesn't look me in the eye anymore. She knows I know.

Most of my contact with Sister Mary's lawyer, Maurice "Maury" Kaplan, is by phone since I don't currently have a residence. Only I *do* have a residence, it turns out. He tells me that an airplane ticket and transportation were to be arranged upon her death. So, I can go to my new home any damn time I want.

Somehow, the freedom of it scares me.

I arrive in Bozeman, Montana, as a dusty young man who just lost the closest thing to a mother he's ever had. His mere existence might be due to a compilation of sins. A work-from-home job has also been arranged for me by Mr. Kaplan, should I choose to take the offer. The estate will provide a laptop and updated wiring of the home for Wi-Fi.

It's surreal. And bizarre. And lonely, until I buy a dog from a neighbor. In Bozeman, "neighbor" means they live five miles away.

Beau is a lovely eight-week-old chocolate lab who loves to run after squirrels, but if he catches one, he runs in the other direction. On the sixth night in my new home, one that's drafty but charming, I sit by a roaring fire and I pull open the accordion folder to search through the documents near the back.

The papers are yellow and torn. I see the tears and the age, and my heart skips a beat. I shake my head because she'd never do that. Not Sister Mary.

I pull them out and see where they were once connected to a larger tome. The paper leaves shake as I hold them. I turn them over and it says it, right there at the top: *For Calling The Mule.*

A separate note is paper-clipped to the first page. "*If you want a fresh start. A new life. It's up to you, Joseph. With apologies and so much love, Mary.*"

I'd like to say that I stare at it for a long time. That it's a hard decision. Instead, I'll be honest. I go to my fridge and get a beer. I silently read the spell three times. I see no instructions that say I need other participants or graveyard dirt or the bones of a black chicken. No special instructions other than "read by the darkness of night".

I look at Beau. "I can do that," I said.

I drink three more beers while waiting for night to fall. My only show of nerves. And when I walk out into the moonlight to read it, the hair on the nape of my neck stands up. The dog whines and runs in circles. Weaving his dark body and his even darker shadow through the tall grass, the felled trees, the dead leaves.

I read the words out loud, and when I'm done, I sit in the dry tall grass still damp from recent snowfall and wonder if it will work. The thump of my heart and the fact that my skin feels like it's trying to crawl off my body tells me *yes, it will*. I take a deep breath and try to make peace with myself.

I pat Beau, who can't seem to get close enough to me. Despite the moonlight, the night seems darker and more dank than when we'd first come out.

"That's a good boy," I say, trying to calm him. "I think tomorrow we might have company."

The dog whines again, but in my head, I'm already planning my first real job, my first time with an unpaid woman, my first time eating at a diner without curious gazes.

It's time for some other poor bastard to be the mule.

CONTENT NOTES

Standard warnings for horror tropes (violence, death, murder) apply to all Graveside Press books.

domestic abuse

Ali Seay (she/her) lives in Baltimore with her husband and kids and the ghost of a geriatric wiener dog who once ruled the house. She's the author of several horror novellas which are usually packed with dark humor and feminine rage. Her shorter work can be found in numerous horror and crime anthologies. When not writing, she hunts vintage goods, haunts used bookstores, tempts folks with books at the local library, and is always down for a road trip. For more info visit aliseay.com

Thank you for supporting Graveside Press and our authors.
One of the biggest ways you can help is to leave a star rating
or a review wherever you purchased your copy!

STAY SPOOKY.

Want merch, membership benefits, and discounts on
Graveside books?
gsp-shop.fourthwall.com

Wanna come hang out with the ghouls?
gravesidepress.carrd.co